SWEET *Juliet*

SYREN NIGHTSHADE

Disclaimers

This story is a work of fiction. Names, characters, places, and incidents are the product of the author's imagination and/or are used fictitiously. Any resemblance to actual events, locales, or persons, living or dead, is completely coincidental.

Potential Trigger/Content Warnings

- Adoption
- Death of a Child *(Non-Explicit, Prior to Story)*
- Strained Family Relationships and/or Child Abuse *(Non-sexual)*
- Suicidal Ideation

I sometimes wonder if cemeteries aren't really the centre of everything, and if the world around us isn't really shaped by the will of the dead. Maybe that's why big cities and small towns feel so different.

With big cities, you have all sorts of people moving in and dying there. The cemeteries are full of different types of people, every single one with their own energy that pushes and pulls in countless different directions. There is no single belief shared by every dead person in those cemeteries. There is no single want or hope shared by every soul lingering there. There is diversity among the living *and* the dead.

Small towns, though, are mostly filled with people cut from the same cloth. Most people think similarly, act similarly, and go to schools that teach the same things that their churches do. And after spending their lives in one place, they die there. All of your neighbours who believed in hard, honest work and being tough and *just getting along* are buried next to you. You live among them in life, then you're buried among them in death. There isn't a lot of fighting about what's right and how the world should look. So instead of moving along at its own pace, the world slows down in small towns. Time gets thicker and heavier, and we're all held back by the inexorable will of the dead. It's *their* town. We're just living in it.

Everything that humans have ever built was built on bones.

I was adopted. My parents adopted me some time after losing a baby. I don't know how long after- it could have been a year, it could have been five. I never asked. It never felt *appropriate* to ask. Their marriage had deteriorated, and my adoption was *(I think)* a desperate bid to salvage their relationship. It worked out pretty well, all things considered. Not for their relationship, of course- using babies to fix a relationship never works. But it succeeded in maintaining the marriage. I don't think my mother and father are necessarily in love, anymore. But they're still married.

More notably, it worked out well for me. Not in the sense that I was given a warm, loving home... although I was extremely fortunate, having been adopted into a comfortable, spacious home where there was always food on the table. It worked out well in the sense that I *had* a home at all, and I didn't have to endure life as a crown ward.

I have always been different from the rest of my family. Every Easter, Thanksgiving, and Christmas, I am surrounded by willowy relatives plucking hors d'oeuvres off of passing plates and raising their voices over the chaotic sound of everyone *else's* voices. Some of them will ask me smalltalk questions. *How is work. How was your drive.* Some of them won't talk to me at all. A couple won't even bother looking at me. I've wondered if it's because they know what I see when I look at them.

I mentioned just now that my parents lost a child before they decided to adopt me. To be clear, I do not know this because they told me; they have never spoken of her. I do not know this because one of my relatives let something slip; they wouldn't dare breathe a word of her. Not in my company, at least. I have never seen any evidence of my sister... no old photos, no baby supplies hidden away in a closet, no birth certificates that haven't seen the light of day in years. If I had been anyone else, I would have had no inkling of my sister's fleeting existence.

I say "fleeting"... That's not fair.

My crib used to shake when I was a baby. The flat white bars would jerk back and forth so violently that I'd wake up screaming and crying. I don't know *how* my parents never heard it. But they were the kind of parents who believed in letting their child cry it out while they went about their business ignoring it. They still are, really.

When I was around two, my aunt- my mom's sister, Candice- got pregnant. I can only assume it was unplanned. She hadn't married my uncle, yet. I don't think she had even *met* him at that point. I can't say for sure... But he isn't in any photos until a few years later. No one tells me anything. Talking about the past is terribly rude, so all I have is what I've been able to deduce on my own. But I know that Candice was just finishing university, and had just been accepted into grad school. Even if she didn't go to grad school, she could have found an excellent position just about anywhere she wanted. And then she got pregnant.

I've never heard anything about my cousin Aiden's biological father. I'm guessing he chose not to be involved.

I think my mother resented my aunt a little bit... Or maybe she resented my mother. But they're fine now. Or at least they pretend to be. And isn't that functionally the same thing?

The first time I saw the little girl in my closet, I thought that maybe she was the baby in my aunt's belly. I thought that maybe the little girl was just staying at our house, waiting in the closet until she could be born and meet my aunt, her mother. But when my aunt brought over a tiny, fleece-swaddled boy that looked more like a bean than another kid, I knew that I was wrong. When Aiden cried, it was loud and high and annoying. When the little girl in my closet cried, it was only half-there. Her wails stretched in and out, like waves clawing at the shore. She banged on the closet doors and her screams sounded like the wind ripping through something jagged. She

6

would cry and bang until I was crying too, and my dad would come in and yell at me, making me cry even harder.

They just told everyone that I had nightmares. But nothing ever happened while I was asleep.

When I started going to school, I wore my hair in braids. Every morning when my mom asked how I wanted my hair, I told her the same thing: *Braids, please.* I had a huge jar of hair elastics- the kind with little plastic balls or soft, sparkly puffs at the ends. I had a hundred different hair ties, in every colour I could think of. I loved wearing different ones every day. I loved decorating the ends of my braids with bright baubles, obnoxious and dainty in turns. I loved it so much that I asked my mom to put my hair *back* into braids every night before I went to bed.

Sometimes, I would lie in bed, waiting for sleep, and I'd feel the girl crawl in behind me. I wouldn't turn around- at first, because I was too scared. I would feel her playing with my braids, turning my baubles over in her little hands. Not long after that started happening, whenever I saw her in the dark corners of my room- watching me or playing with my toys- her long, fair hair would be in braids, too.

It took me weeks to remember not to stop breathing when I heard my mattress give and felt her weight creep in beside me. It took me *months* just to stop feeling afraid of her fingers twisting through my hair.

Over time, I grew to find it comforting.

When she was old enough to know what a name was, she whispered it into my ears in the still dark of my room: *Juliet.*

I told my mother and father about her. They just thought I had an imaginary friend. I don't think "Juliet" was the name they gave her... I have no idea what name she was born into. I only ever knew the name that she picked for herself after she died.

Sometimes, during family gatherings or when Candice would come over and visit, Aiden would join me upstairs while the adults were downstairs talking. He would arrive with some of his own toys- Heaven forbid he show interest my dolls or horses- and we would play together. He was younger than me. But truth be told, I didn't mind spending time with him. I liked quietly escaping reality with another kid. Juliet, however, did not appreciate his presence. I think she was jealous.

He couldn't see or hear her. I'm the only one who's ever been able to do that. But that didn't stop her from taking out her feelings on him. Sometimes a door would slam shut right behind him, and startle him into crying. I was always blamed, of course. Or a toy would be moved a foot or two across the floor, not *quite* where he left it, but just close enough for him to trip over when he wasn't looking. Once, Juliet moved one of his toy trucks just in front of the staircase. He tripped on it and fell halfway down the stairs. He got a couple of bruises and cried for a while. The next few nights were awful- Juliet wept well into the night, banging her small fists on the walls of my closet. Looking back, I think she felt guilty. She just didn't know to make those feelings go away.

A few weeks later, when Candice and her husband visited again, Aiden refused to go up the stairs. He was just a little boy, scared of falling again and still waiting for his child's sense of invincibility to come back to him. His father felt that this cowardice was unacceptable from a five-year-old boy. So when his attempts to convince Aiden to go up the stairs failed, he grabbed his arm and forcefully dragged him up. Aiden pulled and cried the whole way. He was struggling so much that he slipped over the steps a few times. One of those times, he actually twisted his ankle.

I think being dragged up the stairs traumatized him more than actually falling down them. Aiden's an adult now and I've noticed that he still doesn't like going up those stairs.

I have another uncle, Gerry, who works at the auto factory just outside of town. When I was younger, he used to come over to all of our houses and help us with our landscaping. He was like our family's designated landscaper. He seemed to really enjoy doing it. He helped my grandparents with the little pond in their backyard, and planted all of the hedges at my aunt's house. We all have mementos of him scattered through our gardens: neat little birdhouses, hard to find rosebushes, and handmade benches nestled in perfect little spots. He liked to talk about hiking and camping.

I remember the first time I saw Juliet outside. She was sitting on the grass with me. I thought we should have a tea party. I brought out a blanket and my little plastic tea set, the pot so full of juice that it sloshed out of the top and made my fingers sticky. I set all of the pieces up on the blanket, placing them *just so.* Then I poured some juice into both of our cups and took a sip. But Juliet just looked down at her cup and cried.

Later, my mother scolded me for getting my tea set all dirty and covered in juice. Then I cried, too. What was a tea set supposed to be for, if not having tea parties with friends?

When I was twelve or thirteen, the factory Gerry worked at made some changes to how the facility would run. He started working longer shifts- twelve hours at a time- and getting better benefits. He had a family and a mortgage, and the new arrangement helped provide for both. But he stopped talking as much... and smiling. I no longer remember a version of him that wasn't always tired. He doesn't help everyone with their gardens, anymore. I haven't even seen him spending time outside in years.

A handful of times, I've seen him walk up to the window overlooking our backyard. Juliet would be running around outside, skipping between bushes and playing tag with herself, one eye on Gerry the whole time. He would look out into the yard and say something in passing. *"You know a little gazebo would look real nice in the corner, there,"* or *"You ever thought about some coleus to fill out that bed, there?"* He would look out the window for another minute or two, then his eyes would dim and he'd walk away. Juliet always watched him go, a dejected look on her face.

I didn't have many friends to talk to as a child. But I didn't mind. Because I always talked to Juliet. As we grew older, she even started talking back.

I spent a lot of time at family gatherings up in my room. I think everyone assumed it was because I was shy or introverted... which isn't wrong. I don't mind loud noises- I actually *like* loud music. But the overwhelming tangle of so many voices talking over each other at once is too much. I can't focus. I can't think. It makes me feel even lonelier than I would if I were actually alone. So I would go upstairs, down the hall, and into my room to escape. Juliet was often there, but not always. Sometimes, we would just sit in quiet together. Other times, I would read a book and she would sit with me, reading over my shoulder. Or we would listen to music- not too loud, though, or my parents would scold me for hiding and being rude. Sitting alone in my room because I was shy was okay. Actually *enjoying* myself was not.

If she wasn't in my room, she was somewhere else: usually sitting outside in the garden, or standing in a corner somewhere, squeezing herself against the walls while everyone else was oblivious to her presence. She looked sad when that happened. Occasionally, I would see her sitting with one of my relatives. She never said anything. They wouldn't have heard her if she did. She just sat behind them. Silent.

Once, she told me that my parents had wanted a bigger family. They had planned to have a lot of children. I was surprised. It made sense, in some ways. Our house had a generous handful of spare rooms, most of which were called something like an "office" or "sewing room", but were truthfully just glorified storage rooms. But I still had trouble wrapping my head around it. They didn't seem overly affectionate towards children- not to me *or* my cousins. Even more unusually, they didn't seem overly affectionate towards each other. They slept in the same bed at night, but that was all. They never said "I love you", or hugged or kissed each other. Picturing them with three, four, five children felt surreal. Imagining them in a full house, with warmth and affection and a spark of life in their eyes felt uncomfortable.

It occurred to me that maybe losing their first child was what made them this way. I couldn't fully grasp the sheer agony that had to come with the death of a child... I know that I *still* can't. I don't think anyone can comprehend that heartbreak, except for the people who have to endure it every day. And I think that I have even more difficulty understanding because I know Juliet. I seem to have the immense, unjust privilege of gaining what everyone else in my family, my parents most of all, have lost. But being painfully aware of this hasn't dampened my anger with them. *Why don't you just* talk? *Why don't you say something? Why can't you change, just a little bit? Why can't you be real for once?*

I think the feeling of emptiness finally got to me as I became a teenager. I felt untethered, like I wasn't connected to anything or anyone. Except Juliet. I didn't know *how* to connect with anyone. I didn't understand what "connection" even meant.

Juliet felt it, too. After years of peace, she had started crying again. The last time I had seen her cry- *real*, unbridled crying- was when I was a child. It had scared me then, and it scared me again now... too much to sit with her and commiserate. I had my own pain and longing to carry, to learn how to hold without letting it consume me. I didn't know how to share those feelings between us. I only knew how to keep my pain and her pain apart, and that was by keeping *us* apart. And that just made our pain worse.

Juliet went from occasional crying to nightly weeping again. She went back to screaming, louder now than when she was a child still learning how to exist. She had moved on from the sulky banging of walls and onto more destructive outbursts. She would pull the drawers from my nightstand and leave the contents scattered all over the floor. I would leave my room sometimes and find a mug or a glass shattered into pieces across the carpet, having exploded after colliding with the wall. She once slammed my door so hard that it chipped the wood at the bottom. That chip is still there, today.

I couldn't sleep. I was afraid of her again. So I started sneaking out of the house at night and meeting with another group of kids from school.

Sometimes it would be at the empty gravel lot near the bridge. Others, it would be near the woods at the closer edge of town. They would bring mix CDs of pirated music and play it on a portable stereo. Some of them would bring bottles of liquor to pass around. Not all of us drank, but some of us did. They wore ripped jeans, scuffed boots, and jackets covered in patches, pins, and paint. I thought their clothes were cool, so I started wearing them, too. I liked the colours in their hair and how they styled it, so I started mimicking them. I liked the way it looked on me. It was one of the only things I had found that felt good and comfortable. My mother screamed at me the day I came home with a mohawk. Then my father got home and she cried. It made me so angry... the most genuine emotion I had ever seen from her was about my *hair*.

All of the time I spent out at night made it hard to do well in school. I was exhausted all the time. But somehow, I still managed to pass my courses. A lot of us did. Some of us actually got together occasionally to help each other with homework. It was easy for adults to look down on us and believe that we didn't care about anything, or that we were just out to start shit and cause trouble. But we were good kids. We were just dealing with our own problems, in our own way. Just like everyone else.

When my grandmother died, everything became quiet for a while. But only for a while. After a brief pause to get through the funeral, everyone went back to business as usual. At least, they went back to a pantomime of it. No one seemed to cry or yell, or even have the decency to look a little sad. I was young and full of fire and waiting for something, *anything* to crack. But nothing did. I was angry and hurt and *achingly* lonely. I was *desperate* for someone to crack and break with. But I had no one. So when the loneliness overwhelmed my fear, I cracked and broke with Juliet.

I didn't realize how much I had missed her until then. And by the time I did realize it, I missed her too much to be afraid of her.

The kids I spent time with were kind. Flawed, like everyone else. But they accepted me. I called them my friends, and they were. But friendship felt like an ephemeral thing to me. It reminded me of playing with one of those claw machines you find at carnivals and arcades. You move the stick, press the button, and dig into the pile of toys... but the claw only plunges so deep and only stays in the pile for so long. In a second or two, the claw pulls itself out of the toy pile, empty, and the joy fades away, leaving you with nothing. I liked my friends... I was grateful for them. But I knew that our bonds only ran so deep, and that we were only held together by circumstance. Life wouldn't have to try very hard to take us away from each other, and they would forget all about me in due time.

But at least I had Juliet.

She knew all of my secrets. She shared family secrets with me sometimes, since she had so few of her own to give. When I cried, she cried with me. When I was anxious, she would come behind me and run her fingers through my hair, whispering comforting words to me. There was no one I felt closer to than her. She was my sister. She was my best friend.

I felt guilty sometimes, for feeling so alone. *Think of how Juliet must feel. How can you feel so lonely when you have your whole life before you? She is dead. She has no one. But you have her. How can you have the gall to feel alone?*

I went to the beach one day with my friends. I walked into the water as they started chasing each other around. They called to me before I could become too mesmerized by the feeling of the water rippling over my skin. I walked back to the shore to meet them. But I came back later that night, and a few nights afterwards, just to walk back out into the water. It felt like the waves were beckoning. As though they were pulling me in, trying to fold me into the water with them. I looked out across the surface of the water- it almost looked like oil in the dark. I would lay back and float, thinking idly of letting myself sink, wondering how terrible drowning *actually* had to be. And if it truly *was* that terrible, I wondered if it would last very long. A terrible thing is much less terrible if it's brief, I think.

Of course, I had to stop visiting the beach at night when Summer ended and it got too cold.

In all honesty, I've never actually tried to drown myself. Just like I've never actually fallen asleep with my door locked, in a cluttered room with a poorly-placed candle. Just like I've never tried to fall off of the tallest dorm building on campus. I've never done any of those things. Only considered them with idle curiosity.

I can't pretend that a small part of me didn't occasionally feel wistful about it. When I thought about dying, I wondered if I might not be drawn back home afterwards, united with Juliet in a way that I never could have been in life. I don't relish the thought of being stuck in my house forever... But if forever could be spent with my sister, then maybe it wouldn't be so bad. And who knows? Maybe after my parents grow old and die, a new family would move into our house. And we could live in peace with them, as an invisible part of their lives.

Leaving home and going to university was one of the hardest things I've ever done. I wanted to leave. I wanted to run away, live somewhere else where no one knew me. I didn't want to take anything with me. So I didn't. I left almost everything behind and bought whatever I needed new. The only thing I wanted to take with me- the only *person*- was Juliet. But I couldn't. I had to leave her behind, in that miserable house with our miserable family. I felt heartbroken for her, having to stay there alone. But selfishly, I felt even more heartbroken for myself, leaving the person I loved most in the world behind.

When I walked out the front door and climbed into the car, it felt like I was leaving a piece of myself behind.

University was the fresh start that I craved... in theory. I moved to a city a couple of hours from my hometown, where no one knew who I was. The world felt bigger and more real than it had before. *People* felt more real... though maybe I was only seeing what I wanted to see. I studied social work and psychology, and learned about how people think and feel. It made me more conscious of those around me, and more conscious of myself. Somehow, it also made me feel more disconnected from myself. I looked for answers to explain every person in my life, myself most of all. I made new friends, but still felt the same lack of depth and permanency with them that I've always felt. The bonds holding us together were firm enough at the beginning, but would inevitably fray and break with time. Everything is temporary, it seems, except the loneliness and Juliet. But Juliet wasn't there.

I still saw her when I visited home for long weekends and holidays. Then, at least, I could feel *something*. But every other day of my life... there was nothing.

I thought that university would make life feel different. I thought that changing my life so significantly would feel profound or exciting or at least a *little* new. But I still felt empty.

It's been two years since I graduated. Like many of my classmates, I didn't find a job in my field right out of school. I thought about moving back home, back to Juliet. But all that awaited me there were jobs in supermarkets or kitchens or factories. So instead of taking a meaningless, unbearable, minimum-wage job at home, I took a meaningless, unfulfilling job in the city I had already moved into. I didn't feel any affection or loyalty to this place. I just remained there because it seemed like the easiest thing to do.

Part of me thought that, if only I could go somewhere new, look for something that made me *feel* again, that the block in my brain would go away, and I'd be able to feel things like everyone else. I'd be able to experience life instead of just feeling like I'm observing it happen from inside myself. But those *maybes,* those half-dreams, are always followed by something more pragmatic and comfortable: *If you don't feel passionate about something, then you shouldn't do it.* I didn't even try to seek happiness because happiness didn't seem like something you should have to *try* to seek. Happiness seemed like something that should just *happen.* I never looked for anything resembling passion because I didn't feel passionately about finding it.

Normal people don't have to try so hard to be happy.

It took me almost a week of agonizing to apply for a position that found its way into my browser history. It required very flawed and very complicated mental acrobatics: I had to alternately assure myself that this position *could* make me happy, and that nothing would probably come of it, anyways. I found myself having to both feed my hope for change, and assuage my fears of it.

And then I got an interview.

And the more I learned about the job and the organization I'd be working for, the more my hope was fed.

Today, I arrived back home for the Christmas holidays. Lights are laid out over the trees and shrubs of our front yard- *the same lights as every year-* and just enough snow is packed onto the ground to let you know that it's *technically* Winter. I follow my parents onto the porch and into our house. It's already brimming with members of my family, talking over each other in at least four different conversations and picking neat little foods off of gold-rimmed plates. The nine-foot-tall Christmas tree is standing in its usual place by the living room window, domineering in its twinkling regalia. Gifts, both real and decorative, are stacked in careful, cascading piles on either side. I note the urge to inspect some of the real ones, check their name tags, and give them an exploratory shake... One small, comforting rebellion permitted to me that I still indulge in today. I'm sure that there's mellow Christmas music playing from a speaker somewhere. There always is. But I can't hear it over the assault of voices in the house.

I see Juliet standing down the hall ahead of me, near the kitchen. She is beaming at me. If I weren't so empty, I might have cried. I search for the *happy crying* feeling, but there's nothing to find. So I give her a smile instead and I don't cry. It's for the better, really... we don't do that here. It would be rude.

Everyone says hello to me. Some even smile. But no one gets too close. I say hello back. I look back towards the kitchen and Juliet is gone. The pang of her absence hits me hard and starts fading quickly, like the snap of a rubber band. I know where to find her.

I drop my bags off in my room, but I can't stay- not yet. I go back down the stairs, quickly, before I can change my mind.

I find a spot and do my best impression of someone sociable. I no longer receive any sidelong looks- not at the hair, the piercings, or the clothes that were *"probably just a phase"* that I would have grown out of by now. The fact that I ate dim sum last week is now more novel than my appearance. I answer a few questions from relatives about work- *what else is there to ask about?*- and do my best to think of pithy questions to ask in return.

I remember one Christmas years ago, I think I was about fourteen. I decided that, if anyone asked me, *"How are you?"*, I would answer honestly. Just to see what happened. The first time I was asked, I just said I was sad. I don't remember what made me feel that way. Only that I did. The unfortunate cousin who had asked just said something like "Oh," before he shuffled off uncomfortably. The second and final person to ask- my Aunt Candice- just replied with an easy titter and said, "Aren't you a ray of sunshine?" She walked away, and my father, who had overheard the conversation, quickly stepped over to me and hissed, "What is *wrong* with you? It's *Christmas*."

After an acceptable amount of time socializing- forty-five minutes, an hour- I make my way towards the stairs. I try to slow my eager trot to a sedate stroll. My hand grazes the fake pine garland twisting over the banister on my way up. I step into my room and shut the door.

I feel Juliet around me before I see her. Again, crying seems like the appropriate reaction. But I can't. There is a wall between me and crying. There always is, now. We do not say "I missed you," because we already know.

We are sitting on the bed. She tells me of the things she has seen on our street. Her world is smaller than mine. The new neighbours across the street- they've been new for close to two years, now- brought home their baby a few weeks ago.

"They are the *littlest* thing," she says. "Even littler than we were. But they are so... *vibrant*. I can't wait to see them going out for walks. And growing up. I think they're going to be a handful. I can feel it." She smiles as she says this. She no longer grieves the life she will never have.

"It's scary, though," I reply. "Having your first baby premature. Having them stay in the hospital for weeks."

"Hmm," she agrees quietly. "But they're okay."

I think about the neighbours. It makes me feel inadequate and lost. I try to temper my insecurities with empathy. "Still. It's a lot. Just on top of everything. Buying a new house, getting pregnant, getting a puppy *while* you're expecting a baby, then actually *having* the baby premature. That's a lot at once for a young couple."

"Oh, they're not that young. Probably in their... late thirties, early forties? I think."

"Oh." I feel better. I feel her sigh come out as a gentle chill that disperses through the room.

"I can't wait to see them grow up. Especially with a sibling." *She means the puppy.* "I wonder what they'll look like... I wonder if they'll have more children?"

"Maybe."

She makes a contented, speculative sound. "I hope they don't move away."

Something twangs inside me, jarring and uncomfortable. I don't acknowledge it, but my sister knows me too well. She can feel it, too. She doesn't speak... she just looks at me, and I know she's concerned. She knows I will speak when I am ready. I don't know if I will ever feel ready.

"...I applied for a new job a couple weeks ago."

I can feel the air sharpen. "You did?"

"Yeah... I didn't really know whether I wanted to or not. Or if I should."

"What is it?"

I look down at my feet. "It's a non-profit that does a lot of work with children and adolescent mental health." I can feel her swelling in the spaces between my words. "They have a few programs specifically for foster kids, and kids who are waiting for adoption."

"That's beautiful," she smiles. "Why did you question applying for it? It sounds perfect for you."

"I thought that maybe if I didn't feel passionate or excited enough about it, then I shouldn't bother applying..."

Her brow furrows. "It sounds like it would be better for you than your current job, though?"

"Yeah. I think it would be."

"Did you not feel good about it?"

"I didn't feel *bad* about it," I answer. "...I felt positively about it, I guess. Like it was a good opportunity. But..." I shrug. "I didn't feel that excitement you're supposed to have. Or have one of those... 'aha' moments. So I thought that maybe that was a sign. That it just wasn't meant for me."

"Maybe sometimes the right thing doesn't feel like a shock of excitement, or like a puzzle piece fitting into place. Maybe sometimes it just feels like a good idea that makes a lot of sense." I sink back into a pillow as she speaks. "A feeling is just like a goal... If you want to feel it, you need to pursue feeling it. Not just wait for it to happen."

"Well..." *You're probably right. Logically, I know you're right. Maybe one day my heart will catch up to my brain.* "I had an interview with them last week."

"You did?" She smiles again, and it's infectious. I smile, too. I can't stop it from happening. "How did it go?"

"Um. Really good." I have been dreading this moment for days. "They offered me a job."

The light bulbs in my room start beaming, creating a wave of bright light before settling back into their regular luminance.

"That's amazing! I'm so happy for you!" The walls are humming pleasantly. She feels all of the good things that I can't. She feels it for the both of us. "When do you start?"

And this is the moment when I feel myself cracking. I open my mouth to speak, and when I can't, I shake my head, dismissing the words like they've missed curtain call and now it's too late. "I don't know." And in that second, for the fifth or sixth time today, I decide that I can't take the job. It's just too risky. The possible cons outweigh the possible pros. It's just not worth it. "It's in England."

"...How far is England?" Juliet asks softly.

"Too far."

"...But you still applied for the job, anyways." It is not an accusation. It is a prompt.

I feel myself starting to crumble, piece by little piece. I'm suddenly drowning in a cocktail of guilt and hope and regret and need for her approval. "I think... a part of me didn't think I'd get it. And that made applying for it easier. Because I thought that probably nothing would come of it. But I tried not to overthink it, because I knew if I thought too much that I would change my mind and decide not to bother." My voice cracks, just barely. But she knows. "But now I almost wish I hadn't bothered, because now I'm stuck with this awful choice. I feel like no matter what I choose, it's going to be the wrong choice. Because I don't feel like I've *ever* made any right choices."

In the quiet between us, I can hear my family still moving and talking over each other downstairs. Spontaneously I think, *they are happy without me*. In the past, that thought would make me sad. But now it feels very *matter-of-fact* and reassuring.

"Is it because you like where you are now?"

"You mean where I live? Or where I am in life?"

"Either."

I sigh. "I don't know. No. Not really. Moving was a nice change, when I went to school. But it's lost its novelty, now that I'm out. I don't *hate* it there. But I don't feel any strong desire to stay, either. And my job-" I give her a look. She understands. "It's not what I wanted. I'm not *happy* with it... But I've never been truly happy with anything."

Have I? What *is* genuine happiness supposed to feel like? I often think that maybe I *have* felt it. Maybe what I *think* is happiness is actually just an idealized fantasy that only exists in my head. Maybe I imagine emotions that don't actually exist. Maybe I'm just making myself miserable by chasing something imaginary. Maybe this is just as good as it gets. And I'm only numb and sad because I can't accept that.

"Do you think that you might be happier if you take the job?"

"I don't know. Maybe. Maybe not." *Maybe I'm too broken to be fixed.*

"Do you think it's more likely that you'll be happy in England than you will be here?" she asks cautiously.

"...Possibly... Yeah, I guess. *Technically.* But probably it won't make any difference at all."

"Okay." I feel her move off of my bed, and in a moment she is on the floor below me. "Do you think you'll feel more content in England? Not happy. *Content.*"

I sit there silently. It would be putting my education to use, for the first time ever. I would have more opportunity to grow and advance. The non-profit had mentioned potentially paying to further my education if they kept me on, which meant that I could get a Master's or a PhD, and all of the opportunities that came with them. Moving to a new country felt like a new start- even more so than university had. I would know absolutely no one. And no one would know me. It would be extremely freeing... and isolating.

But I already feel isolated here. I *don't* feel free.

Juliet speaks again. "If it's not that... then what's keeping you here?" I look at her. Her eyes are sad. She already knows the answer, or at least suspects. I don't want to say it out loud. I think that maybe it will feel smaller if I lead with the minor reason instead of the major one.

"...I think it would make everyone sad. Or upset them. Or just... make them unhappy." It feels stupid when I say it out loud. Stupid, but true anyways. "They wouldn't understand. They wouldn't even *try* to understand. They'd say it's ridiculous to move across the world to a job that doesn't even pay that much-" but still, it's enough- "and to a place where I have no one. Why bother going through all the trouble of moving when I can find something that pays just as much here?" I have to remind myself not to raise my voice too much. "And why go so far away that I can't visit whenever I want?" *Here we go.* "I mean, maybe they'll say all that and more to my face. In their self-righteous, passive-aggressive way. Or maybe they'll say it behind my back. I don't know which one is worse. But I'm sure one of them is going to happen. And... maybe they'll be sad if they don't see me. They might be hurt. My choice will be *hurting* them. I will be causing them *pain*."

It wasn't about the rest of my family, anymore.

The tears start coming. Because it's about Juliet. And it's about me, too. Juliet starts crying a little bit with me, and it's all I can do to hold myself back from full-blown sobbing.

"Listen to me," she whispers. "You are *not* responsible for their reactions."

"But I still have to deal with the consequences of them."

"You will have to deal with them no matter what you do. Whether you choose to go and deal with their reactions, or choose to stay here and deal with the resentment of missing this chance because of them... You will have to deal with *something*. Either the consequences of moving forward, or the consequences of holding yourself back."

I slide off the bed and join her on the floor. We are huddled together with our backs against the mattress, leaning into each other.

"You're not responsible for their emotions. You're not responsible for their happiness. Only for the pursuit of your own."

"But what about you?" I feel her shake her head, "If I leave-" *leave*. I don't think a word has ever sounded so cruel. "-I might not be able to see you. For I don't know how long. With anyone else, I could text. I could email. I could call. But you and me can't do that. With *anyone else* in this family, I could handle the possibility of not seeing them for years at a time. But not you." I search for her hand. She gives it readily. "I don't know if I can do that to myself. I don't know if I can do that to you."

She would be stuck here. Left behind, in this small, small world with a small, small group of people who don't even know she exists. Maybe it would be peaceful... Or maybe it would be unfathomably lonely. Maybe she would find a way to move on without me. She would get so lonely that she'd decide to fade into nothingness while I was away, and I wouldn't even know until I made my way back. I would have no way of communicating with her. She could be happy and doing wonderfully. She could be angry or sick with despair. She could be struggling. She could be dead- really, truly dead- for years. And I would have no way of knowing.

She squeezes my hand, as if she knows what I'm thinking. I often believe that she does. *Any time I see you could be the last time. This Christmas could be the last time.*

But isn't that true for everyone I know?

"I don't think I can do it."

I feel her hands on my face, like the sun has just started shining on the skin there. She looks into my eyes, seeing through me in the way she only does when we're sharing secrets or making the most solemn promises.

"You *need* to go out and live your life. You only have one chance to live it." The tears are already evaporating on her cheeks, but mine still haven't stopped. "You already have enough inside you trying to hold you back. And so much inside you trying to push you forward. Don't let anyone or anything *outside* of you try to hold you back, too. Not even me."

"But what if it hurts too much?"

"Then I will always be here. Even if years pass, and the world moves on, and everyone else in our family is dead and gone...

I will still be here. Waiting for you. And if one day we have to say goodbye, we will say goodbye together."

I put my arms around her, and we sit holding each other.

My sister. My best friend.

"I love you."

"I love you."

Later, I clean away all evidence of my tears and go back downstairs to join the rest of my family. I stand at my bedroom door and look back at her one more time before I go. This evening, I will respond to the non-profit and accept their offer. I will get started on my work visa and moving preparations after Christmas is over and I've arrived back at my apartment. I will not tell my family until then. For the next precious few days, I will spend as much time as I can with my sister, talking and laughing and sitting in the cozy silence together, just cradling this secret between us. The day before I leave her, she will tell me to *fly*. And when I get on the plane to London, I will move with caution, careful not to disturb the fresh tattoo on my arm: a sparrow and a rose- a *Sweet Juliet*. It will remind me of my secret sister, my always home. It will remind me of the decision I made to let go. It will remind me that happiness, whatever it may be, is worth pursuing.

Syren Nightshade *(she/her)* is a Canadian author, dancer, singer, actress, and performing artist. She has an affinity for Gothic fiction, and frequently explores themes of feminine rage, longing, & duality in the pages of her work.

She wrote *Sweet Juliet* after making the decision to come out to her family.